THIS CANDLEWICK
GAMEBOOK
BELONGS TO:

YOUR TASK

Your task is to rescue your five friends and
then find your way out of the Castle of Fear.
Each time you choose a new route, you
will be told to turn to a different page.
But the wicked wizard has set many traps
in the castle. Sometimes you can avoid them by
finding your way through a maze or by finding
something hidden in the picture. Often you have
to use your wits. All you have to help you is
a magic wish that you can use only once.
Your sole companion is a monkey named Zetto
who is not always very helpful. Whatever happens
you cannot turn back. Good luck!

Text copyright © 1986 by Patrick Burston
Illustrations copyright © 1986 by Alastair Graham
All rights reserved.
First U.S. paperback edition 1996
Library of Congress Cataloging-in-Publication Data
Burston, Patrick.
The Castle of Fear / Patrick Burston ; illustrated by Alastair
Graham.—1st U.S. paperback ed.
Summary: While rescuing five friends and then finding the way out
of the Castle of Fear, the reader chooses among various routes
and thereby controls the course of the story.
ISBN 1-56402-860-7 (paperback)
1. Plot-your-own stories. [1. Rescue work—Fiction.
2. Castles—Fiction. 3. Picture puzzles. 4. Plot-your-own stories.]
I. Graham, Alastair, ill. II. Title.
PZ7.B945535Cas   1996
[Fic]—dc20   95-50788
2 4 6 8 10 9 7 5 3
Printed in Mexico
This book was typeset in Galliard.
The pictures were done in watercolor and ink.
Candlewick Press
2067 Massachusetts Avenue
Cambridge, Massachusetts 02140

THE CASTLE of FEAR

PATRICK BURSTON

ILLUSTRATED BY **ALASTAIR GRAHAM**

CANDLEWICK PRESS
CAMBRIDGE, MASSACHUSETTS

Here is the wicked wizard's castle. The drawbridge is down and the guard is fast asleep. This is the perfect chance for you and Zetto to slip unnoticed into the castle.

Now which way?
If you choose the left-hand
passageway, turn to page 8.
If you choose the right-hand
passageway, turn to page 10.

A cracked tile gives way as Zetto
touches it. All of the cracked tiles are
really trap doors! Find a safe way across
the courtyard to one of the staircases.
(Trace a path with your finger.)

Turn to page 12.

Turn to page 14.

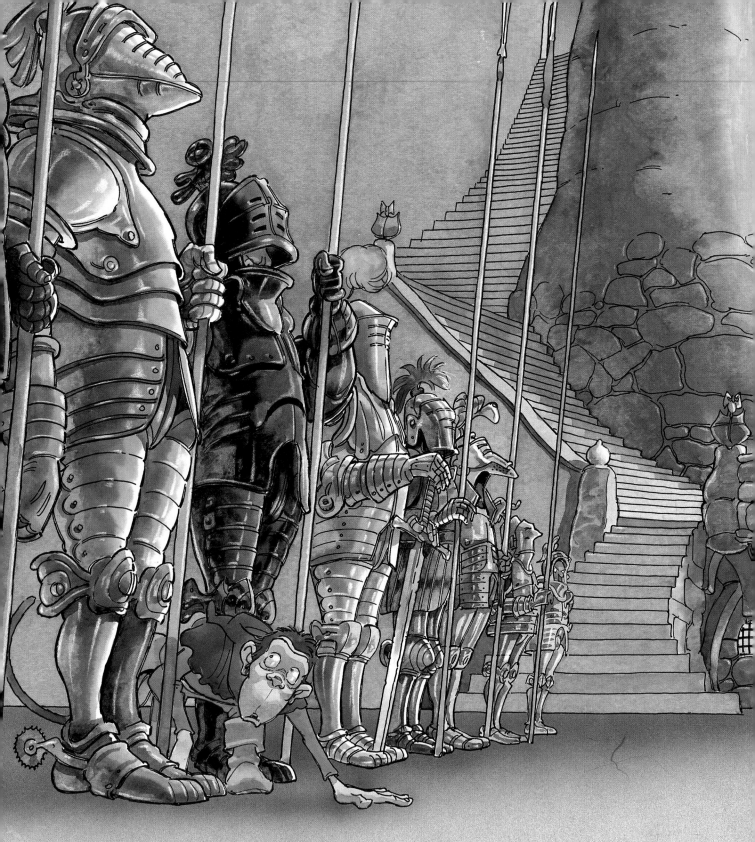

Careful! Guards are hiding in five of these suits of armor. Only by figuring out which ones and avoiding them will you be able to pass through the room.

Then, if you choose to go up the staircase, turn to page 14. If you choose to enter the banquet hall, turn to page 16.

The stairs are blocked by eight terrifying ghosts conjured up by the wizard. You can only conquer them by matching each up with its evil twin.

If you continue
down the stairs,
turn to page 18.
Or use your magic
wish, and turn to
page 20.

You are trapped in a turret! What can you find in the pile of junk that will help you get across to one of the towers?

If you reach the tower with the pointed roof, turn to page 20.
If you reach the tower with battlements, turn to page 22.

A delicious-looking feast! But the wizard has set many traps. Can you find the eleven dangers you should avoid? Then proceed carefully.

If you decide to take the stairs behind the table, turn to page 22. If you take the stairs on the right, turn to page 24.

Five skeletons! Could they be your friends?
Before you go on, study their bones closely.
What can you find to prove that each
is not human?

If you choose to go up the stairs into the left eye socket, turn to page 28. If you go up into the right eye socket, turn to page 26.

You and Zetto are being attacked by vampire bats. Since they are afraid of light, find something to break open the windows.

If you go down the stairs,
turn to page 28.
If you go through the door,
turn to page 30.

Five ghastly creatures are slowly inching their way up the walls of the tower. There's a bow handy—can you find one arrow to kill each creature?

Now which way? If you decide to dive into the moat, turn to page 32. If you choose to climb down the rungs, turn to page 30.

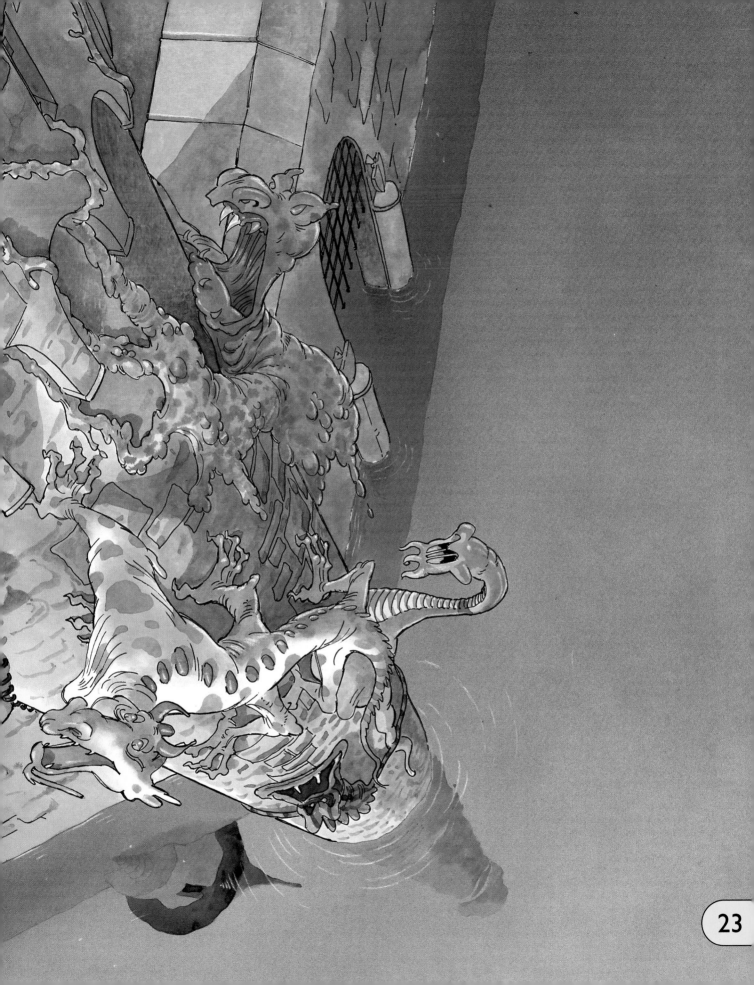

What a view! But the wizard's victims can't enjoy it because they have been turned into stone gargoyles. You will become a gargoyle, too, unless you smash the only uncarved stone. What can you use?

Now which way?
If you choose to go through
the door, turn to page 34.
If you decide to dive into
the moat, turn to page 32.

If you choose to go through the door, turn to page 34. If you decide to dive into the moat, turn to page 32.

Here are your five friends,
imprisoned in a horrible
torture chamber! Find the five
keys needed to release them.

You have now released everyone,
but can you lead them back
to safety? Which way?
If you take the tunnel,
turn to page 44.
If you take the stairs,
turn to page 36.

You have discovered a mechanical monster created by the wizard. Three of the four wires that activate him are broken. However, one wire is still connected to a switch. Find it and turn off the power before the monster kills you.

More confusing stairs! Which way should you go? If you take the left-hand archway, turn to page 38. If you take the right-hand archway, turn to page 42.

Poisonous fumes suggest that it would be fatal to fall into this treacherous chasm beneath the castle. Find a safe way across it. (Trace a path with your finger.)

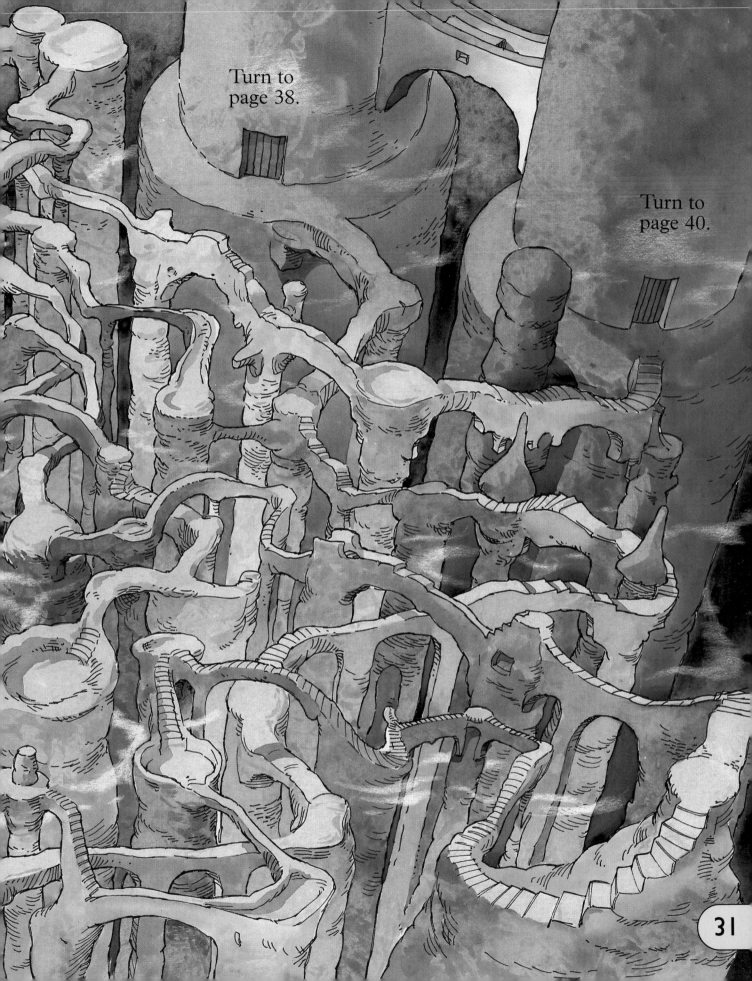

Turn to
page 38.

Turn to
page 40.

The castle guards have seen you
and Zetto dive into the moat!
Find something to breathe through
so you can swim underwater.

If you swim into the tunnel and
climb up the steps, turn to page 42.
If you swim farther inside the tunnel,
turn to page 40.

You and Zetto are held by the spell of a magic mirror. You must find nine differences between the image and its reflection in order to be freed from the spell.

Then step through the doorway reflected in the mirror and turn to page 42, or go through the real doorway and turn to page 38.

Disaster! Your friends have been recaptured and you have been thrown into a dungeon with thirty starving rats. Find a hungry cat for every five rats and you will be safe. But you must go back to page 7 and start again in order to fulfill your task.

The wizard's pet dragon has set fire to the floodgates that hold back the water in the moat. Can you figure out a way to avoid drowning? (Grab some treasures as you float away!) But you still need to rescue your friends, so go back to page 7 and start again.

Face to face with the Slime Serpent!
Can you see how to trap it in its
watery pit forever? But you still
have to rescue your friends, so go
back to page 7 and start again.

It's the wizard himself!
He's angry because Zetto
has stolen his wand. And he can't
find his pet toad. (Can you?)
While the wizard is distracted,
use the wand to transport Zetto
and yourself back to page 7
and start your quest again.

You've finally escaped from the castle! But there are wolves ahead, gathering to howl at the full moon. Choose a path that will get you safely to the village.

YOU ARE
SAFE IN
THE VILLAGE
AT LAST!
YOUR TASK
IS DONE.

Answers

14
Throw the rope and hook
across, keeping the rope taut
by tying it to one of the iron
rings, and cross hand over
hand on the rope.

16 – 17
- burning fuse on cannon
- bomb in boar's mouth
- snake under dish cover
- musket in portrait
- candle burning through rope
  will release spiked chandelier
- poison in wine bottle
- live tiger
- trap door under chair
- dagger under table
- poisonous mushrooms (fly agaric)
- deadly spider

18
- horns
- six fingers on each hand
- hoofs
- tail
- three feet

20 – 21
an ax

24
a mallet and a chisel

32
You can use one
of the hollow reeds.

34 – 35
- Zetto's medallion
- carved helmet on banister
- bat's head in arch
- pattern on beam
- shape of beam support
- battlements outside
- color of sky

- fire in torch
- carpet on stairs

38
You can hop
into the barrel.

40
Pull the chain to
dislodge the rock so
the stone slab falls
on the iron grille.